Bramble and Maggie

HORSE MEETS GIRL

Jessie Haas

illustrated by Alison Friend

CANDLEWICK PRESS

For Nancy Gallt, with love and more love
J. H.

For my dad, who loved to paint horses
A. F.

Text copyright © 2012 by Jessie Haas
Illustrations copyright © 2012 by Alison Friend

First paperback edition 2013

The Library of Congress has cataloged the hardcover edition as follows:

Haas, Jessie.
Bramble and Maggie: horse meets girl / Jessie Haas; illustrated by Alison Friend. — 1st ed.
p. cm.
Summary: Bramble the horse gets bored giving riding lessons, but regains
her enthusiasm when she goes to live with a girl named Maggie.
ISBN 978-0-7636-4955-5 (hardcover)
[1. Horses — Fiction.] I. Friend, Alison, ill. II. Title.
PZ7.H1129Br 2012
[Fic] — dc23 2011018625

ISBN 978-0-7636-6251-6 (paperback)

12 13 14 15 16 17 SCP 10 9 8 7 6 5 4 3 2 1

Printed in Humen, Dongguan, China

This book was typeset in Dante.
The illustrations were done in gouache.

Candlewick Press
99 Dover Street
Somerville, Massachusetts 02144

visit us at www.candlewick.com

CHAPTER ONE

Bramble

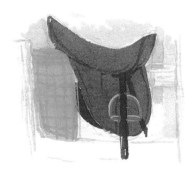

Bramble gave riding lessons.

Mrs. Blenkinsop told the rider what to do, and the rider told Bramble what to do. They went around and around the riding ring with the other horses. Around and around. Around and around.

One day Bramble started to walk more
slowly. She dragged her feet in the dust.
All the other horses passed her.

"Bump her with your legs," said
Mrs. Blenkinsop. "Make her speed up."

The rider bumped with her legs.
Bramble sped up, all right. She trotted
past the other horses.

"WHOA!" said Mrs. Blenkinsop.
Bramble stopped.

"Take a deep breath," Mrs. Blenkinsop told the rider. "Now ask her to go forward."

The rider asked. Bramble went backward. All the way around the ring.

"Oh, boy! This is not a good lesson," said Mrs. Blenkinsop.

The next day Bramble gave another
lesson. She didn't do anything to scare this
rider. She didn't do anything at all.

"I see," Mrs. Blenkinsop said. "You are
bored, Bramble. Too much going around in
circles. But riding lessons are supposed to
be boring for horses. Try to put up with it."

The next day, another rider got on her.
Bramble lay down. She closed her eyes
and groaned.

"I get it! I *get* it!" said Mrs. Blenkinsop.
"No more riding lessons for you.
You need a person of your
own to have fun with."

A person of her own. Bramble liked that idea. But not just any person. She would have to be picky.

A family came to look at Bramble. "She seems like a nice safe horse," the mom said. "We have a ring at home. Amy can ride her there."

A ring was just what Bramble did not want.

Amy got on Bramble's back. Bramble trotted around the ring, fast, and faster, and even faster. She was careful. She did not let Amy fall. But she did not slow down until she was ready.

"She has her little ways,"
Mrs. Blenkinsop said.

Amy's mother said, "She is not the horse
for Amy."

The next family wanted a jumper.
"Bramble has her little ways,"
Mrs. Blenkinsop told them. "But she
loves jumping."

That was not exactly true. Bramble
could jump if she wanted to. She did not
want to very often.

The boy got on Bramble's back.
Bramble walked to a jump. She pushed
it over with her nose.

"Bramble is not the horse for me,"
the boy said.

CHAPTER TWO
Maggie

"Did you see that sign?" Maggie asked.

"Yes," Mom said. "I was hoping that you didn't."

"You always say horses cost too much. But this horse is free."

Dad said, "Lots of horses need good homes these days." He turned the car around.

"But you can't ride it today," Mom said.

"You don't have your helmet and boots."

"Yes, I do!" Maggie said. "I take them
everywhere, just in case."

Mrs. Blenkinsop said, "I am thrilled that you want to look at Bramble. Come with me to meet her."

Mom whispered, "Maybe this horse is free because there is something wrong with it. Don't fall in love too quickly, Maggie."

"That could be a problem," Dad said. "Maggie is in love with all horses."

That was true. But Maggie had her big

horse book with her. She took *it* everywhere,

too. Quickly she opened it.

"Maggie, this is Bramble," Mrs. Blenkinsop
said. "Bramble, meet Maggie."

Uh-oh! Maggie thought. When she looked
at Bramble, she did not feel picky. She liked
Bramble's color. She liked her eyes. She liked
the way Bramble looked back at her.

Bramble felt as picky as ever. Maggie
seemed like a pleasant girl, but maybe there
was something wrong with her.

Maggie got into the saddle. She rode
Bramble around the ring, and around again.
Bramble started to go faster. Too fast.

"Sorry," Maggie said. "My mistake. I didn't
mean for you to go that fast." She tightened
the reins, asking Bramble to go slower.

Bramble went slower.
So slow she almost
stopped.

"Oops," Maggie said. "I didn't mean *that* slow." She squeezed with her legs, asking Bramble to go faster. *I am making a lot of mistakes,* Maggie thought. *But she is very nice about it.*

Bramble turned her head. She looked hard at Maggie. Then she went around the ring again. Not too fast. Not too slow.

"Wow!" Maggie said. "I finally got it right!"

Bramble tossed her head and snorted.

"I mean *we* got it right."

"Could I try her outside?" Maggie asked Mrs. Blenkinsop. "I don't have a ring at home."

"Go ahead," said Mrs. Blenkinsop.

Maggie rode up and down the long
driveway. Bramble put her ears forward.
She had a bounce in her step.

"You like this better, don't you?" Maggie
said. "Me too. Do you want to come live
with me, Bramble?"

Bramble turned her head again.
She looked at Maggie.
Very gently, she bit the toe
of Maggie's boot.

"Is that yes?" Maggie asked. "I hope it's yes. We will explore. I will show you the ocean, Bramble. And I will take good care of you. I hope I don't make too many mistakes."

Maggie got off. "Bramble is the horse for me," she said.

"Remember," Mrs. Blenkinsop said, "she has her little ways."

"Don't fall in love with the first horse you see," Mom said. "It says so right here."

Maggie took the book. Bramble nudged it out of her hands. It fell open on the ground.

CHAPTER THREE

Big Snake

Maggie spent a week getting ready for Bramble.

She fixed the garden shed into a stall.

She hung up a net and filled it with hay.

She hung up a bucket and filled it with water.

She made a deep bed of shavings.

When Bramble came, Maggie put her in the new stall. "I will leave you to get used to it," she said. "That is what the book says."

The stall was square and clean. Bramble was used to it in two seconds. She tasted the hay. Perfectly acceptable. She tasted the water. Sweet and clean.

But outside she saw blue sky. She smelled grass. Green grass. Juicy grass. Delicious grass.

Bramble whinnied.

Maggie ran back.

"Are you used to your stall already?
I will show you the yard."

Maggie showed Bramble the lawn first.
It was delicious.

"Now come see the backyard," Maggie
said. She led Bramble around the house.

Bramble saw a dark shape. She stopped.
She stared.

34

"I know horses see differently from people," Maggie said. "But a bush is a bush, no matter how you look at it. You are not afraid of a bush!"

Bramble sniffed. She tasted.

Of course she was not afraid of a bush.

In the backyard a strange animal was eating the lawn. It was taller than Bramble. It had long, thin legs.

Bramble raised her head to see better. She lowered her head to see better.

"That is only a swing set," Maggie said.
"See? I'm not afraid!" She slapped the swing
set. It sounded like metal.

Bramble still did not know what a swing
set was. But it was not an animal. It would
probably not jump at her.

"Brave Bramble!" Maggie said. "Come on."

Then Bramble saw it. A snake. A BIG snake.
It stretched all the way across the yard.

Bramble stopped. She snorted. She stamped
her foot loudly.

The snake did not move. It was not afraid. But Bramble was.

Not Maggie. She picked it right up and said, "See? It's just a hose. You're *not* afraid of a hose!"

Bramble wasn't afraid of a *hose*. She was afraid of a snake. She still didn't go one step closer.

"Bramble, look," Maggie said. She squeezed the snake's head. It hissed. Water sprayed and made little rainbows.

A hose. Bramble took a drink. Then she bit the hose, just to remind it not to turn back into a snake.

CHAPTER FOUR

Good Night

Maggie stayed with Bramble all day. She brushed Bramble and braided her mane. She leaned on the stall door and watched Bramble nap.

When it got dark, Maggie went inside to eat supper. After supper she came back out to watch Bramble eat *her* supper.

Before bedtime, Maggie gave Bramble

more hay and kissed her on the nose.

"Good night, Bramble," Maggie said.

"See you in the morning."

Maggie could not sleep. She lay in her bed, wide awake. She thought, *I have a horse!* Then she thought, *Did I fill her water bucket? Yes. Did I fill her hay net? Yes. Is her bed nice and comfortable? I hope so. I have a horse!*

Bramble could not sleep. She stood at
her stall door, wide awake. She was alone in
a new place, with no other horses. With no
Maggie. It did not make her feel sleepy.

The house lights went off. It was quiet.
Too quiet.

Bramble knew what to do about that.
She turned around. She kicked her door
with both back feet.

BANG!

She kicked it again. *BANG-BANG!*

Lights went on in the house. Maggie
came running.